The Goose Girl

A Traditional Chinese Tale

retold by Marilee Robin Burton
illustrated by Valerie Sokolova

Scott Foresman

Editorial Offices: Glenview, Illinois • New York, New York
Sales Offices: Reading, Massachusetts • Duluth, Georgia
Glenview, Illinois • Carrollton, Texas • Menlo Park, California

Ting's father worked for a well-to-do landowner on
a rice farm. He toiled in the rice paddies from early in
the morning to late in the day. Ting's mother was also
busy all day, working in the kitchen. And Ting had her
own chores to do. She tended to the geese.

Even though the family worked hard, they could
afford only a tiny hut and meager meals. But Ting
never complained. She did not envy the wealthy girls
of the town with their silk sashes. She was happy with
her life.

She dearly loved her mother and father. Her only wish was to bring greater happiness to them.

Each morning Ting set off to work just as her parents did. She gathered the landowner's geese from their pen behind the landowner's home. She guided them to the little pond and would sit and watch them. In the afternoon she would bring them back up the hill to their pen.

One day, as she walked behind the honking flock, a large gray gander suddenly took flight. Ting watched as the goose flew across the pink morning sky. "What freedom!" she thought. "If only I could fly like that! I would touch the sky and take a handful of sunshine for my mother. I would chase the wind and bring its secret back to my father."

Ting could not stop thinking of the gander flying through the morning sky. All day she pictured him far above the muddy earth. She wished she could fly too. The more Ting thought about flying, the more she began to believe she really could fly. If only she tried hard enough, she was sure she could fly just as the gander did.

Ting knew she would need wings in order to fly. Perhaps the pond water where the geese swam might help her grow wings! She bent down at the water's edge and scooped up a handful of the cool water. She patted the murky water onto each shoulder. Then she began to flap her arms, waiting for wings to sprout.

Moments later the landowner's daughter walked
by and saw Ting flapping her arms. She stood a
moment in silent bewilderment before bursting
out laughing.

"You silly girl," the landowner's daughter called
out in a loud voice. "What in the world do you think
you are doing?"

Ting humbly told her about her wish to fly like
the gander.

"Oh, a goose girl can't fly!" said the landowner's
daughter with a scoff. She was not a tactful girl. She
laughed once more and left Ting standing by the pond.

Back in her own big house, however, the landowner's daughter began to wonder. Could a girl really grow wings?

"If anybody around here is to fly, it should be me," she said. "And not a poor, silly goose girl. Who is she to fly? I have pretty clothes. My father is rich. Pond water, indeed!"

The landowner's daughter took a small pitcher of milk from the kitchen. She poured some milk into each palm and patted it on her shoulders. Then she went outside and began to flap her arms.

At that very moment the daughter of the town judge was strolling on a nearby bridge. The sight of the flapping girl caught her by surprise. She felt a sense of bewilderment just as the landowner's daughter had when she first saw Ting.

"What in the world are you doing?" asked the judge's daughter.

"Why, I am going to grow wings and fly," the landowner's daughter answered. She stopped flapping long enough to tell the judge's daughter the story.

"Humph," said the judge's daughter with scorn. She quickly left the flapping girl alone.

"Ridiculous," she said to herself. The landowner's daughter was wrong to think she could fly!

If anyone could fly it would be the daughter of a judge! Who could be more worthy than she? She was rich. She was pretty. Her robes were made of silk.

"Milk, indeed!" said the judge's daughter. "Scented oil would be best!"

And with that, she slipped into her mother's room for a few drops of perfumed oil. She rubbed the oil onto her shoulders. Then she went outside to flap her arms.

When the princess passed by in the afternoon with her royal procession, the judge's daughter was still flapping. The princess stopped. She sent one of the servants to ask the girl what she was doing and the servant soon returned with the tale of sprouting wings. The princess bowed her head and giggled, signaling the procession onward.

But, just as with the other girls, the princess herself could not resist the story.

"The judge's daughter is silly to think she can fly!" said the princess. "Flying is for royalty. And I am royalty. If anyone were to grow wings and fly, it would be me. Scented oil, indeed!"

Once back at the place she had her servants bring her the finest jasmine perfume. She asked them to pat it on her shoulders. Then she went out to the courtyard and flapped her arms.

The story spread throughout China. and before long, every girl was flapping her arms. Every girl was waiting to sprout wings and soar. Some had sprinkled milk onto their shoulders. Others had used scented oil. Still others tried fragrant perfume. Only Ting, the goose girl, had been content with murky pond water. Her only wish was to search the sky for some secret happiness to return to her hardworking parents.

Each girl thought she should be the one to fly. Each girl was sure that she was the most deserving. Each believed that all the others were less deserving. But Ting was the only girl not thinking about herself. She only thought about her mother and father and the happiness she hoped to give them.

One morning Ting stood by the pond, flapping her arms as she had been doing for days. But on this morning, something unusual happened. Geese began to gather around Ting. Before long, she was surrounded by geese. As she stood flapping her arms, the geese picked her up. Ting soared into the sky with the geese. At last she could go in search of the wind's secret and a handful of sunshine for her parents!